The Crystal Stair

The Crystal Stair

CATHERINE FISHER

Barrington Stoke

First published in 2016 in Great Britain by
Barrington Stoke Ltd
18 Walker Street, Edinburgh, EH3 7LP

www.barringtonstoke.co.uk

Text © 2016 Catherine Fisher

A CIP catalogue record for this book is available
from the British Library upon request

ISBN: 978-1-78112-542-7

Printed in China by Leo

Contents

Chapter 1
Pyramid

From the roof of the Girls' Tower, Caz could see all of the Settlement. She sat on the bench with both her hands round a mug of hot chocolate and gazed out.

The white Pyramid rose opposite her. Beyond were the Boys' Tower, all the Tech Halls, and then the family houses. She could see the glass walkways that linked the buildings, the leafy trees of the park, even a glimmer of the lake and the regal black swans that lived on it.

If she stood up, Caz would also see the green hills of the Outlands and the fields where the bio-crops grew.

And if she narrowed her eyes against the sun, she would even see the terrible bright sparkle of the distant Ice.

Instead Caz sighed, and sipped the chocolate. She and Will had been in the Settlement of World's End for three months now, and she was still trying to get used to the place.

All these people! She had never known so many people. There were over 6,000 of them, all those who had survived the Blue Star.

She stood, walked to the rail and looked down. The streets were not like the frozen City she had escaped from. Here they were clean and new and lined with young, fresh trees.

It was warm and safe here in the Settlement. She should be happy. But she wasn't. She was restless and uneasy. And deep in her heart she knew why.

"Caz! *Caz!*"

Will's shout rang up. From far below, he was waving at her. She waved back, put the empty mug into the waste chute and hurried to the lift.

The Girls' Tower was five storeys high and every girl over ten who had no family of her own lived there. When the Blue Star had rained down its deadly poison, most of the survivors had been children, because they had been fast and fit and healthy. Their parents had not been so lucky. So these two Towers were huge orphanages. Caz didn't like the place. She had her own room on the fourth floor, and it was nice to have clothes that fitted, but they were dull, and every girl had the same. Dark green trousers. Dark green shirt.

Boring.

The lift door opened. Caz hurried to the security desk and ran her hand over the fingerprint reader. The machine said "Exit allowed" and the door opened.

Will was waiting outside. He was wearing the blue uniform of the Tech Hall with a badge that read *Level 1 Trainee*. "At last!" he said. "I've been here ages."

"Have you got it?" Caz asked.

Will frowned. "Yes, I've got it," he said. "But it wasn't easy. If they find out, I'll be in real trouble."

"They won't." Caz turned. "Let's go now."

"Caz, listen!" Will put out an arm to stop her. "We shouldn't be doing this. It's always the same with you! Why do you always have to break the rules?"

Caz glared at him. "I need to find out about my father."

"He's not here," Will said. "We know that."

She walked away fast, her face hot, and Will had to run to catch up. For a moment neither of them spoke. Then Will said, "As soon as we arrived, you asked at the Pyramid about him. They checked. He isn't here."

"I want to see for myself."

"You have to face it, Caz. He died when the Star came, back in the City. Like thousands of others."

Stubborn, she said, "I know he's alive."

"You don't know. You just want it."

She stopped and looked at him. "OK. *OK!* You may be right. But he worked for the government, Will. They had bunkers under his office block. Safe places, in case of an attack. He must have gone down there. I just want to see the records for myself. That's not much to ask, is it?"

Will sighed. He must have known he wouldn't talk her out of it. Once Caz had an idea she never let it go.

"Well, we'd better do it now," he said. "I've got two hours before I have to be back at class."

In front of them rose the Pyramid, a huge crystal building in the white emptiness of the central square. This was the Settlement HQ, where all the information that had survived the Blue Star disaster was stored.

As they walked up the broad white steps, Will changed the subject. "Have you decided what work you'll choose yet?"

Caz shrugged. "They've told me. It'll be at the hospital. We need doctors."

Will looked surprised. But Caz was right. In this tiny, enclosed world everyone had to do what the Settlement needed. Choice was a thing of the past.

The doors slid open.

The Pyramid was a vast emptiness, all white, with a glossy floor of black tiles. As Will and Caz crossed the space, they felt tiny, their shoes tapping on the reflected lights, as if they walked across a starry sky.

Caz had discovered that the oldest records were kept here, the ones written down in the panic and chaos of the days just after the Star. They were in a vast room called the Hall of the Lost. She had to see those. Maybe something there would help her.

They took the lift to the third floor. A white corridor faced them, lined with doors. They walked down it with rapid steps. One or two people passed them, and one woman looked at them curiously, but she said nothing.

Will and Caz turned the corner.

"That's it," Will said.

The Hall of the Lost had a tall double door with a security slot near the handle.

"Try it then," Caz said. "While there's no one around."

Will nodded. He looked round, then took out a card. Caz stared at it. The clear plastic was invisible until he held it up, then in a rainbow shiver she saw numbers printed deep inside.

"Are you sure it'll get us in?" she asked.

"One way to find out." Will slipped the plastic card into the slot.

The door made a soft snapping noise, and the light on the lock turned from red to green.

Will pulled the door open and they slipped inside.

"Wow!" Caz said.

The Hall of the Lost reached to the very top of the Pyramid. Above them the crystal roof came to a sharp point. Hundreds of white butterflies fluttered in and out of the open windows of the apex.

The air smelled sweet and musty.

All around were shelves of books and boxes and papers. Thousands of them.

Will groaned. "Where do we even start!"

For a moment, Caz shared his dismay. Then she noticed each section of the shelves had a letter above it.

"L," she said. My father's name is Richard Lewis. So it has to be L."

As she hurried away between the shelves, Will stared after her.

"All those years living as kids together in the Store," he said, "and I never knew your surname."

The shelf labelled "L" was thick with dusty files. Caz grabbed one and flicked through it, but the names were all strange to her and nothing was in any sort of order.

She threw it down and took another. "What a mess! All this should be sorted out."

"There's a job for you then." Will was turning pages. "Caz, these aren't just lists of people. It's all sorts of stuff, anything saved from the City, and the other places."

She nodded, in despair.

Millions of files, business records, archives from lost schools, whole libraries of books, endless computer print-outs, pictures, letters, notebooks, magazines … all the written stuff that anyone had brought to the Settlement had been dumped here, waiting to be sorted and ordered.

But no one had done it.

Caz threw down another file in frustration. "This is crazy. Surely ..."

"Shh! Listen." Will turned, eyes wide. "Someone's coming. Quick!"

But it was too late.

The door opened.

Chapter 2
Vault

Caz froze.

A woman stood in the doorway. She was middle-aged, a little bent over. Her steel-grey hair was cropped close to her head.

She seemed astonished. "What on earth are you doing in here?" she asked. Her voice was low but angry. "How did you get in?"

Will looked at Caz, a flash of panic. "The door was open, so we just ..."

"Rubbish." The woman took a step closer. "I keep this place locked tight, that's my job. I'm calling Security."

Her hand moved towards a button on the wall. Her finger was already on it when Caz gasped. "Wait. Listen, please! We're new here. We don't know all the rules yet."

The woman's finger paused on the button. "Well yes, I know that. You're the two who flew here from the City. Everyone was amazed. We didn't think anyone was left alive in there, in the Ice and the poisoned air."

Caz took a step forward and held out her hands. "Well, we were. We lived for years in a department store with some others. They're here too now. A squad went back in for them."

"Yes, but that doesn't explain …"

"I want to find my father," Caz said. "To find out what happened to him."

The woman was very still. Then she breathed out. Her hand moved away from the button, just a fraction, but Caz saw it. She took her chance and went on. "I thought there might be something here to help, but it's all just in so much of a mess …"

The woman's face crinkled with irritation. "You don't have to tell me!" she said. "It'll take years to sort. Decades, maybe."

Suddenly she dropped her hand and turned to a narrow door. "Come on. This is my office. Maybe you can take a look."

Caz flashed a grin at Will, who blew out his cheeks in relief.

The office was stacked with papers. The woman waved them to a seat. "My name's Lee. Lee Anderson," she said. "I'm in charge of this hall. Well, I've taken charge of it. No one else cares."

Caz sat down, but Will stayed standing.

"I thought everyone was needed in Tech?" he said. "If the Settlement power goes down this whole place would be frozen over with ice in days. Keeping the power on is more important than sorting old papers."

Lee shrugged. "I know. I work on Plant 32 most days. But look at me. I'm not much use." She grinned as Will went red, as if he'd been thinking the same thing. "On my time off I potter round in here," she explained.

"Why?" Caz asked.

"I like it. All the old stuff. It's an archive." Lee sighed. "I worked in a museum, before the Star came. I hate to see all this disorder. We mustn't forget the past. It's important."

Caz leaned across the table. "Can I try to find my father's name?"

Lee frowned. Then she turned to a narrow counter and switched on a kettle. "I'll make us some tea. And you can try."

It took Will and Caz hours – the tea Lee had made them grew cold at their side. They went through thousands of names and histories, story after story after story, checking every list Lee suggested. They learned that many people had made it out of the City alive, but the early days of the Settlement had been hard. Many had died in the bitter snow and ice, or from the terrible sicknesses the Star had caused. Most of the lists were a jumble of words, scribbled in haste, with names crossed out or changed.

At last, Caz got to the end of the huge file and turned the page.

It was blank.

"And that's it?" she said.

Lee came over. "That's all the survivor information I've been able to sort," she said. "You haven't found him?"

Caz shook her head. She was too devastated to speak. She had always known there was only a small chance that her father might still be alive, but to take in the fact that he was really dead hit her harder than she'd thought. She could remember him so clearly – a tall man with thick dark hair and a loud laugh. Big hands that had picked her up and tossed her in the air and caught her.

Will said, "You have to face it, Caz."

Silent, she nodded, and stood up.

"Thanks for your help, Lee," she said. "And the tea. Sorry we broke in."

Lee looked almost as unhappy as Caz. As they went to the door she said, "You can come back and try again. And I'll look myself if I have time. Remind me, what was your father's name?"

"Lewis. Richard Lewis. He was a chemist."

Lee had her back to them, with a pen in her hand to jot it down. But the pen did not move.

For a moment she was completely still.

Then she turned her head, and there was a gleam of pure astonishment in her bright eyes. "*What did you say?*"

Caz stared. "You know him! You know that name?"

Lee sat down in the chair. "Oh dear. Oh Lord. This changes everything," she said. The words were quiet, almost as if she was speaking to herself.

Caz ran back to the desk. "Tell me!" she begged. "Is he alive? Have you seen him?"

The room was silent. Only, from far above, the barely heard flutter of a thousand white wings against the crystal of the windows.

Will said, "You do know something."

Lee put her fingers together in a tight knot. She looked up. "All right. I have come across that name. But it was in a file so secret it's not supposed to exist any more. They told me to destroy it. But I kept it. Like I said, I think the past should never be lost." She stood up. "Come on," she said. "You should see this."

She walked ahead of them back into the main archive, past a maze of shelves and cluttered desks, to a spiral stair that ran up to a gallery. Caz walked behind, her heart pounding. She didn't even want to speak to Will. All she wanted was to hug that sweet, delicious knowledge to herself, that her father's name was here, somewhere. That he had made it out of the City. That he was in the Settlement!

Lee came to a door that she opened with another of the plastic access cards. This one was edged with red. The door was heavy and very thick. It reminded Caz of the doors to bank vaults in old crime films she had watched in the Store.

Beyond the door was a tiny space, lined with pigeon-holes, all stuffed with papers. Lee took a thin file out of one, turned and held it out.

The file was black with a square white label on the cover.

The label said

THE DRAGONFLY INCIDENT

and below that, in untidy writing, was a single word.

Destroy.

As they all stood and looked at the file a bell rang.

It was far off, outside the building, but its urgent, harsh sound was unmistakable.

It was the curfew bell, the bell that told everyone to report home.

"Take it with you," Lee said. "Hide it, and when you've read it bring it back, but don't let anyone know. Especially the other girls in the Tower. I should have destroyed it and they'll punish me if they find out I didn't."

Caz clutched the file tight to her. She nodded, but Will said, "What do you mean, *punish* you? Who will? The Council? I thought this place was safe."

When Lee spoke her voice was strangely amused. "You're new here," she said. "Be careful. Things are not as simple as you think."

As she said it, all the lights began to dim.

Lee swore, pushed them out of the vault and slammed the door shut.

She turned, and there was a thin film of sweat on her forehead. "Listen!" she hissed.

Caz froze. Heavy steps were coming along the corridor outside.

Lee looked round, her eyes full of fear. "In here. Hurry." She unlocked a door and pushed them through it.

Will gasped and Caz nearly cried out. It was a fire escape. All at once they were outside, high on a metal balcony clinging to the side of the building, a thin ladder zig-zagging from it down the roof of the Pyramid.

"Go!" Lee hissed. "I'll be slower than you ..."

"Wait." Caz stopped her slamming the door. She put her eye to the crack and looked back into the room.

A tall man in a dark uniform had come in and was standing there, gazing round. His face was smooth and intent. His hair was the lightest of blonds – almost white, cut close around his head. She saw how he listened, then he crossed to the vault and checked it, tugging at the lock.

Caz shivered.

The man turned.

Maybe he felt a draught, or sensed her there.

Instantly Caz closed the door with the tiniest of clicks and raced down the sloping ladders after Will and Lee.

They used Lee's set of plastic cards to slip back into the building on the floor below. They took the lift to the ground floor, walked out and hurried away, but it wasn't until the Pyramid was out of sight behind the Towers that any of them felt safe.

Will stopped, out of breath. "Wow," he gasped. "So who was he?"

Lee shook her head. "I don't know. I've never seen him before. There must be some silent alarm in the vault and when we took the file out we triggered it." She looked worried. "You will hide that file?" she said. "Maybe I should take it back ..."

"Not before I've read it." Caz held it tight. She wasn't giving it up now. She looked down at the label. "What was the Dragonfly?" she asked.

Lee frowned. "A plane," she said. "A plane that flew off into the Ice on a rescue mission. And never came back."

Chapter 3

Emergency

Caz lay awake in her narrow bed.

The room was dark. All the voices and echoing sounds of the other girls in the Tower had stopped at least an hour ago, but still she waited, staring up at the shadows on the ceiling.

The bed was warm, but there was shivery fear in her heart. She wondered if there were hidden cameras in the building. Had the sinister white-haired man found out the *Dragonfly* file was missing? Was he searching for her, even now?

However much Caz told herself not to be stupid, the ice-cold fear stayed lodged in her heart.

The file was hidden under the blankets with her. When she moved, it crackled. She couldn't wait any longer.

She sat up and switched on the light beside the bed. She had dumped a pile of her clothes at the foot of the door, so no light would show from her room, and the door was safely locked. She took out the file from its hiding place and opened it.

All around her, the Tower was absolutely silent, the girls in the rooms above her and below her deep in sleep.

She began to read.

The file was a mess of documents. Some of it was just numbers and lists, other pages were so full of technical stuff she had no clue what they were about.

Then Caz came to a report dated almost two years ago.

At 12.00 hours on 17.12.29 the following emergency message was received from

Shadow Valley Deep Mine, approx 60 miles north of the Settlement. The transmission was poor. Contact was broken and could not be re-established.

Recording follows.

There was a small 'play' symbol embedded in the page. Caz pressed it.

A buzz of static came out, so loud she had to scrabble to turn the volume down. Then, faint and far off, a woman's voice, crackling with fear.

"This is an emergency! Repeat, emergency. This is Shadow Valley. Please, can anyone hear me? Oh God, you have to help me! I'm the only one left. The others are all dead ... the ... breaking through ... new tunnels in Shaft J. Monsters ... horrible ... their eyes ... blind ... Can you hear me? Answer me!"

The terror in the woman's voice held Caz rigid. Behind the voice were other sounds, booms and echoes, static bursts that exploded, and once a weird high singing note that made her shiver.

The message was really breaking up now, making almost no sense at all. Caz strained to hear it, holding the file close to her ear.

"The Eternum has to be ... We have to ... frozen."

And then a horrible shriek of panic.

"The crystal stair!"

A loud crackle.

Silence.

Caz breathed out. For a moment that utter fear and sense of the frozen Ice had been right here, in her warm, safe room.

Outside her door a small creak sounded in the building.

Caz barely heard. She was fascinated by the file. It told her that Shadow Valley was a copper and mineral mine, far out in the Ice, one of the network of outposts that were needed to supply metals to survivors of the Blue Star.

What had happened there? Was it some sort of attack?

She turned over. The next page was headed

SEARCH AND RESCUE TEAM 1 sent in response to emergency call.

Aircraft – DRAGONFLY Ex D55 Military convoy.

<u>Crew</u>
Alice Rees – Pilot
Clifford Henson – Navigator
Fran Lopez – Medic
Richard Lewis – Scientist

There it was – her father's name!

Her heart pounded in her chest and she couldn't keep still. She jumped out of bed and paced around the room, reading as she went.

The search and rescue team had been sent to find out what had happened at the mine and so the *Dragonfly* had taken off late that afternoon.

But what had happened to them, the rescue party?

She tore through the papers.

- Lists of supplies, safety protocols.

- Weather reports on the depth and thickness of the Ice.

- Report on the mine.

There had been seven people at Shadow Valley, but not one of *Dragonfly*'s calls to the mine had been answered.

Then there were a few recordings of the pilot's voice. Caz listened to them eagerly, hoping she might hear her father speak, but there was only the pilot. The other members of the crew were just murmurs in the background.

The pilot gave ordinary flight reports. The *Dragonfly* had flown for three hours over the frozen world, she said. Then she had spotted the buildings of the Deep Mine, and she had brought the plane in to land.

Caz listened to the recordings.

"*SART 1 to Settlement. We have visual contact with the target, over. Hard to make out. The fog is really heavy here, but there seem to be buildings jutting out of the Ice. Frozen solid. No sign of life. No lights. How should we proceed, over?*"

Another voice answered, a man's voice.

"*Settlement to SART 1. Only go into the mine if you think it's safe, over. We don't want to lose you. Be sure to wear full protective gear. Send Richard and Fran in. You and Cliff stay with the* Dragonfly. *Any trouble, take off at once. Repeat. Abandon mission if there's any threat. None of us know what's happened in there.*"

"*Understood,*" the pilot said. "*The team is going in now. Over.*"

Caz kept the recording running as she paced the room in a fever of excitement.

Ten minutes passed. Half an hour. There was nothing on the recording at all. It was as if they had never spoken again. And then, in a burst of static so loud it made her jump, the recording came back on, half way through the pilot's scream of terror.

"Oh my God! What is that!"

A crackle and buzz of static. Then nothing but silence.

A sharp knock at the door made Caz gasp.

"Caz? Caz, are you OK? What's going on in there?"

She swore, jumped up and shoved the jumble of papers under the bedclothes as best as she could.

Then she slid open the door.

Holly from the room next door stood outside in a pink T-shirt and shorts. She stared eagerly past Caz into the untidy room.

"Sorry," Holly said. "I thought I heard a shout. And someone walking up and down. Hey, have you got a boy in there, Caz? I mean, you know it's not allowed ..."

"I had a nightmare," Caz snapped. "That's all." She opened the door wide so that Holly could get a good look in. "Sorry I woke you up."

"Oh, that's OK." Holly's whisper was soft. "As long as you're all right."

"I'm fine. Good night."

Caz shut the door, then stood with her back against it. She listened as Holly went back into her room, and the door closed, slow and reluctant.

Caz stood, gathering herself.

She was breathing as hard as if she'd been running for miles, and she knew why.

It was fear. A fast beat of fear.

Not of Holly, but of whatever had made the pilot scream out like that.

Far out in the Ice, something had come up from that mine.

She combed through the file over and over again, but that was it. Nothing. Just one neat piece of paper pasted into the back.

No more messages received.
Dragonfly *presumed lost.*
No further action.
File closed.

Caz threw herself down on the bed, and glared up at the ceiling.

There certainly *would* be further action. And she'd be the one to take it.

Chapter 4
Theft

"That's so scary," Will said.

He took out a pen and wrote the words on the paper napkin that was wrapped around his coffee cup. "*My God! What is that?* That's what she screamed out?"

"Yes."

"She must have seen something that scared her stiff." Will shuddered. "And then nothing? You mean the whole expedition was never heard of again?"

"So the file says."

"Weird." Will looked round the canteen, busy with Settlement workers on their morning break. "Weird and scary." He glanced at Caz.

She was staring back at him, and he knew exactly what she wanted.

"No chance!" he said. "They'd never allow us."

"I'm not asking anyone's permission." Caz's voice was low and fierce. "We're getting a plane, Will, and going out there to see for ourselves."

He sighed. "I suppose it's no use talking sense to you? Caz, we can't just steal a plane. And even if we did ... we don't know where this Shadow Valley is."

"It's all in the file," Caz told him. "I need to know what happened, Will. And if you don't want to come, I'll go on my own."

She got up and strode off.

Will stared after her in dismay. "Caz. Wait!"

A few people looked up.

Will caught up with her at the door, and they went through. Outside the Tech building was a small garden, a circle of glossy grass surrounded by golden flowers. The white butterflies that were everywhere in the Settlement fluttered here in clouds.

Caz was walking fast, but Will just folded his arms and said, "If you don't stop and talk to me, I'm going back in."

Caz stopped and turned.

Will was smiling. "You're an idiot," he said. "Did you really think I'd pass up an adventure like this? Of course I'm coming with you."

Caz grinned.

"*But* ..." Will said before she could speak. "We have to do this carefully ..."

"If we tell anyone, they won't let us go."

"I know," he said. "But it's the Ice, Caz. We have to be prepared. It'll be beyond freezing out there. Have you forgotten what that's like?"

She hadn't. Even after their months in the Settlement, she could still feel the terrible numb cold of the world outside. "We need proper clothes, then," she said. "Supplies. Food. There must be stores of them somewhere."

"I'll find out. Being in Tech has its advantages." Will came closer. "We'll need weapons, too."

Caz was silent. A sudden chill of fear had struck her, as if that scream of terror from the recording had slashed with crystal sharpness across her memory.

What had happened out there?

"He's dead, isn't he? My father?" It was a whisper.

"Probably," Will said, gently. "The cold would have ... And if he was OK, why didn't he come back? Or any of them?"

She looked up. "We'll make sure. I'm not leaving him out there."

But, even as Will nodded, Caz wondered why no one else had gone to look. Was it a lack of resources? Or were the strange mines of Shadow Valley more sinister and dangerous than anyone could have imagined?

Will knew it would be no use trying to steal a plane from the main hangars, so that night, after curfew, he checked out the repair yards. It was dark, and no one was about, but he was still wary. He knew there would be cameras.

Most of the aircraft in the repair yards were in pieces, but at last, after an hour of hunting, all on its own in one corner, Will found a small dock with a cover over it. He took the cover off and saw a sleek red micro-ship.

It was freshly repaired and ready to go.

The name on its side was *Ladybird*.

He smiled.

Perfect!

Caz still had the cold weather clothes she'd worn from the Store in her room. They were even more battered and grubby than she remembered. Food was more difficult, but with her Tower pass she blagged some extra hot packs and warm-up stir-fries, saying she wanted them for a birthday night in the Girls' Tower. It wasn't much, but it would have to do.

Caz rushed back to her room with the food. As she came out of the lift she stopped, gasped in dismay, then stepped back in at once and pressed the button.

The doors slammed shut.

Caz swore.

A man had been coming out of her room!
A tall man, with short, white hair, carrying
something under his arm.

The lift whooshed up. Caz slipped out, ran to
the railing and looked down. A shadow moved
in the darkness. Then, as he walked down the
stairs, she saw him clearly.

There was no doubt about it. It was the same
man they'd seen at the Pyramid.

She let the lift go down, then ran to her room
and let herself in.

Everything was tidy, just as she'd left it. So
what had he taken?

She ran to the desk, jerked the drawer open
and hissed in fury.

The black file was gone.

Caz stared at the empty drawer and anger
and despair welled up inside her. How dare
they? How could they pretend this had never
happened? Her father and the rest of the
Dragonfly crew were lost out there, along with
the miners of Shadow Valley.

Didn't those deaths matter?

Burning with anger, Caz shoved the food and water into a bag and grabbed her coat and full Ice kit. She slammed the door so hard behind her that Holly ran out to see what was happening.

"Caz?" she cried. "Where are you going?"

Caz fixed Holly with a glare and shut the lift doors in her face.

Once she got outside, Caz ran. She bumped into Will just as he was coming out of the repair yard.

"It's all set," he said. "I've programmed the plane and we can go tomorrow, first light …"

"We have to go now!"

"Caz. I've got a class in –"

"Listen!" She grabbed his arm. "That man with the white hair's been in my room. He took the file. They *know*, Will! If we don't go right now, they'll stop us! We'll never get this chance again."

Will stared at her. "Are you sure?"

"I *saw* him."

A bell rang. Workers put down their tools next to the planes they were working on and headed to a low building. Cooking smells drifted in the air.

Will breathed out. "OK," he said. "Come on, it's over here."

Caz grinned. Will was a planner, but he was always quick to adapt.

They walked between the planes. The red micro-ship stood alone in its corner. They stripped the cover off as fast as they could and climbed in.

"I'm pilot," Will said firmly.

"OK! Just hurry!"

"Activate," Will said in a strong voice, and all the controls lit. The plane began to move. It taxied between the larger aircraft, gathering speed as it left the hangar and emerged into the open air.

Night was falling. The controlled temperature of the Settlement had cooled. A few bats flitted over the icy glitter of the stars.

Will checked the fuel and instrument status. "Prepare for take-off."

Caz looked back and saw people running out from the hangar, shouting after them. "Just go," she shouted. "Quickly!"

But already the plane was roaring down the runway, the g-force pinning her back in her seat until she could barely breathe.

And then they were flying.

Chapter 5
Ladybird

There was a red spotted insect on the control panel of the plane. A logo of some kind. Caz thought it must be a ladybird. She had never seen a real one. Maybe none had survived the Blue Star.

Now she leaned her head against the window and looked down. Far below, the landscape was dim and dark green. The plane droned over the black outlines of a forest and then a river, the water a glint in the darkness.

Will had set the *Ladybird*'s autopilot function and had fallen asleep, curled up in his seat, but Caz was too excited to close her eyes.

The moon rose. Its silvery glow lit Caz's face and eyes, and now she could see her breath, a soft shimmer of cloud.

They had come to the edge of the Settlement's weather control.

The Ice began with small white patches – a rime of frost on a sloping field, a scatter of snow turning a dark hilltop frosty white.

The white patches joined. And suddenly the plane was flying over an immense ice-field that stretched stark and white to the horizon. The shadow of the *Ladybird* on its surface was the only moving thing in the world.

Caz sighed. Everything down there was frozen. Every blade of grass and every tree, every fox and badger, every person. There had once been villages and towns – she could still see the top of a church steeple jutting from a mass of ice, but the rest was buried deep.

She didn't want to think of it, but it haunted her. The Settlement was alone, isolated, a tiny warm spot in a frozen landscape. And the rest of the world was dead, destroyed by the Star.

Well, that's what she'd been told. But maybe, somewhere, there were other Settlements. Far off in the highlands of Scotland, or the mountains of Wales, or across the furthest plains of Europe.

Maybe in the hearts of ancient cities, like Paris or Vienna or Berlin, people were still alive.

If only there was some way of helping things live and grow again.

She shivered.

The cold was starting to bite.

Her breath misted the window and turned at once to a fur of tiny crystals.

Will muttered and shifted in his seat.

Caz flicked on the heating. From now on, they would die without it.

When Caz woke, a voice was calling her name, sharp and urgent.

She opened her eyes and saw Will, watching her. But it wasn't him who was speaking.

"*Caz Lewis. Will Hart. We know you can receive us. Answer please.*"

"It's them," Will said gloomily.

"Turn it off."

His hand went out, then he said, "Maybe we should let them know where we're going."

"So they can come and get us? No way." Caz leaned over.

"*This is Settlement Control*," the voice said. "*Turn around and come back. Your journey is unauthorised and you are heading too far out of the Weather Zone. We insist on your response, over.*"

Caz was silent.

Then the voice changed, became hard and clear.

"*Caz and Will. Listen to me. I know where you're heading. I know about Shadow Valley Mine.*"

Caz's finger paused on the button. "You!" she said. "You're the man who took the file!"

Silence. Then, "*Where you're going – it's dangerous. Turn around or I will ...*"

"No! We'll be back when I find out what happened to my father. And not before."

She cut the comms channel before he could answer.

The plane flew on into the darkness.

After a while, Will said, "They might come after us."

Caz felt herself flush with guilt. "I'm sorry," she said. "I've dragged you into danger. I've been selfish."

Will laughed. "Nobody drags me anywhere, Caz. I wanted to come, remember?"

She smiled back. Then she sat up. "Look! Down there. See?"

A dark stain lay on the Ice like a patch of spilled oil. For a moment she thought it was liquid spreading out, but then, as Will inclined the plane, the moon shone on it and they knew it was frozen hard, whatever it was, and the darkness was a deep red, turning the Ice to a patch of blood.

"Weird," Will muttered. "Look, there's more."

The land was rising to a range of jagged peaks. A glacier glittered in a long, serpentine valley.

"Is this it?" Caz muttered. It didn't look like a mine, even in the dark.

"The nav guide says it should be."

Will checked the controls again, then turned the plane and circled down towards the Ice.

They landed softly, the wheels skimming and bouncing on the frozen surface. The *Ladybird* bumped and slid to a halt.

Outside the plane, everything was black. Not even the stars were visible now, only a faint sheen of moonlight.

"Nothing," Caz whispered. "Nothing."

She stared out into the Ice. The eerie moonlight played tricks with her eyes. It caught on ice edges and shattered crystals. It glittered like jewels in places, but when she looked the glitter was gone.

"We'll try the radio first," Will said.

He switched it on. "*Ladybird* to Shadow Valley Deep Mine. Can anyone hear me? Over."

Nothing but a low crackling hiss of static.

For a moment they listened to it, then Will said, "Hopeless." He reached out to turn it off.

"Wait." Caz grabbed his hand. "Turn it up."

"But ..."

She turned the volume up. The static was so loud that Will winced, but Caz bent nearer, listening hard. She'd thought she heard a whisper, something soft, a slither behind the crackle and hiss of white noise.

"Is there anyone there?" she whispered.

Nothing.

Will snapped the sound off. "Come on," he said. "Let's get out and take a look. Or maybe ... maybe I should go and you stay here. One of us should stay with *Ladybird* in case –"

He stopped. Caz was freezing him with a look he knew only too well.

"Right," she said. "Then that'll be you."

"No chance."

They both grinned.

The cold weather gear was awkward to struggle into in the tiny cabin, but at last they were suited up.

Caz said, "OK?"

"OK. Let's go."

She cracked the door seal. Instantly the cold crackled in. Caz shuddered with the shock of it. It reminded her of the day they had left the confined world of the Store and entered the City, but here the cold seemed even worse.

Caz's gloves sent showers of frost flying as she climbed down the ladder of *Ladybird*. Will followed. They stood still and looked around.

Bleak winds gusted over utter desolation.

Around them were the frozen outlines of dark buildings, encased in glassy ice. The wind blew scatters of snow across the surface of the Ice. It rippled with an uneasy whisper.

Mist lay low over it all, like a ghostly veil.

The cold was intense, but the silence was worse. And there was a smell, a faint tang in the air like metal.

Caz breathed out a cloud. "Over there," she said.

She had seen something small and bright, something that glittered. As they crunched towards it over the frozen surface, she slipped and slithered. Will came behind, even more awkward.

The Ice was broken and bubbled. In places it gave way, and Caz's feet slipped down into cracks. She prayed that none of them would be so deep they'd swallow her whole.

The small, bright fragment shone in the moonlight. When Caz came to it, she reached down and brushed the Ice away. It was a piece of smooth metal, rising up.

"What's that?" Will whispered.

Caz shook her head. Wind whipped hair across her visor as she crouched down and wiped away more snow.

Then she gasped.

The metal was the edge of a door. It was ajar, frozen open in the Ice. Its curved shape looked like the door of a plane.

With a murmur of frozen breath, Caz began to scrub fiercely at the Ice. Will watched for a moment, then jumped down to help her.

It took a few seconds to clear enough snow, then Caz said, "There!"

She tugged a torch out from a pocket and flashed it on. Its cone of light was bright and deep. In the seamed Ice they saw the perfect outline of a word.

DRAGONFLY.

Will stared. "It's their plane! The search and rescue team."

Caz was too tense to speak. She leaned closer, pushing her face right up against the frozen surface, straining her eyes to stare in. The torchlight was fractured and broken by the Ice, but Caz could see a bank of controls, spilled food packs, a pen frozen and snapped in half.

And then a hand.

An eye, looking up at her.

She jerked back, with a cry of alarm.

"What?" Will said.

"The crew. They're still in there."

Chapter 6
Crew

Will pushed Caz out of the way. "Don't look!"

"I need to see."

She crouched next to him. She felt sick with nerves, empty, as if all her energy had gone in a second.

Was her father here, in this plane, buried deep in the Ice?

There were two people in the cockpit, a man and a woman.

One glance told Caz that the man was not her father. She gasped in relief.

The bodies were frozen rigid in their seats – the woman with her eyes closed, the man staring up almost defiantly at whatever he had seen last.

There were no visible injuries.

"So what happened?" Will muttered. "Disease? Suffocation? An attack?"

"But who would attack them?" Caz asked. "Maybe it was just the cold ... the plane's systems went down."

Will shook his head, frustrated. "If only we could get inside ... But there's no chance, even with the picks. The whole cockpit's rock-hard with ice."

Caz was glad. She stepped to one side, out of the line of sight of the dead man. His blind stare was unnerving her.

"OK," she said. "So they must be Alice, the pilot, and the other man ..."

"Cliff."

"Cliff. OK. The others – Fran and my dad – they went into the mine." She looked up at the windswept desolation. "That's where we need to go."

Will didn't answer, so she turned.

He was bending over the seal of the cabin, his gloves brushing at the Ice. His face was so close to the metal that his visor bumped against it.

"What the hell's this?" he whispered.

He lifted his glove. A long thin trail of slime, silver as a snail's, hung from his fingers.

They both stared at it in disgust.

"How on earth is that not frozen?" Caz said.

"No idea. It's everywhere."

Caz felt sick, but she forced herself to look. As the moonlight glinted on the strange silvery slime she saw that it was all over the Ice and the trapped plane and, as she moved back in horror, she saw it glisten on her sleeve and her boots.

She scrubbed her arm in clean snow. "Yuk. It's disgusting."

Will seemed to agree. He too scrubbed at his glove in the snow, then backed off.

Caz turned again to the mine. "We need to go in. But the plane ..."

She couldn't say what she was afraid of, because she wasn't even sure what it was. All she knew was that without *Ladybird* they would be trapped here. She had no idea if anyone from the Settlement would ever come out looking for them.

Will shrugged. "You're not going in there alone."

"Will ..."

"We have to take the chance. I mean, who's here to damage the plane? No one."

He sounded confident, but as Caz looked over the eerie, moonlit darkness of the lost mine, she shivered. The wind gusted the Ice in rasping swirls, making a sound like the constant whisper of tiny voices.

And what had left those silvery trails of slime? Some horrible, crawling thing?

"Come on," she said. "Let's lock the plane and go."

But first they took half of the food and water, leaving the rest hidden in the cockpit. Will belted on the gun.

"Watch you don't blow your foot off," Caz muttered.

He glared at her. But Caz was secretly glad they had it.

They trudged over the frozen surface towards the low line of buildings, stooping as the wind rose and whipped snow in their faces. Ahead, the moon was low, sending stretched shadows behind them. Every hollow and hillock of the Ice seemed huge and inky black. If anything was hiding here, they'd never see it.

Caz told herself there could be nothing alive in this cold. But, as she slipped and slithered, she had to fight the desire to stop and stare round. She had the strangest feeling that someone – something – was watching her.

Maybe Will felt it too, because he muttered, "Over there. See?"

The nearest building was just a dark roof jutting out of the Ice. But, in its shadow, something moved.

Will ran clumsily towards it and Caz ran after him, but when she got there he was standing and staring at a door that was banging softly in the wind.

"Left open," he said.

"For all this time?" Caz moved past him to drag the door wide. The entrance was blocked with thin slabs of ice.

"Where's your ice-pick?" Caz said. "We could smash this."

Will laughed. "Well, we could try."

The Ice was nowhere near as thick as they'd thought and it soon shattered under the blows of the ice-picks. At last, a black hole into darkness was revealed.

Before fear – or Will – could stop her, Caz crouched and crawled in. Light from her torch lit her way until she emerged into some sort of control room.

Maps and charts on the walls were solid with icicles, and whatever had been on the table was frozen in an icy slab. Filthy blinds hung at small, square windows. Papers and files and boxes littered the floor.

Will ducked in beside her. "What a mess."

"Too much of a mess," Caz said. "As if there was some sort of fight."

"Maybe."

Will's torch beam flickered, as the ice crystals caught it. He crossed over to one of the maps and scrubbed ice from it. As he studied it, Caz listened.

The only sound was the endless gusting of the wind and, behind that, tiny as the scratching of mice, the soft fall of the snow.

"Caz."

"What?"

"We're at the entrance to Shaft J. Wasn't that ...?"

"Yes!"

She remembered. The recording came to her in a flash, the terror in the woman's voice.

"Oh God, you have to help me! I'm the only one left. The others are all dead ... the ... breaking through ... through the new tunnels in Shaft J. Monsters ... horrible ... their eyes blind. Can you hear me? Answer me!"

"This is it," Caz said in a whisper. "The place where it happened. Something terrible came up from underground and ..."

"That's not likely, is it?" Will said. "Monsters? Get a grip, Caz."

Caz wished Will wasn't so logical – it was annoying. "I hope you're right," she said.

"I am," he said. "But I wish we had some sort of breathing kit. It's a mine, so there must be plenty here, but who knows where." He turned. "Do you want to go on?"

"Of course I do."

He grinned. "Why did I bother asking?"

The map showed that a door to the left led to Shaft J. They went through and walked down a corridor, crunching over the frozen floor. It was good to be out of the gusting wind, but the tunnel was dim and eerie and Caz felt closed in. The tunnel led them to a lift shaft, the door a simple metal grid that she caught hold of and pulled aside.

They looked down.

The shaft was pitch black. Cold air rose from it.

It probably went down for miles.

Will looked at the large red and green buttons on the wall. "Well," he said. "It's worth a try."

He pressed the green button.

At once, far far below, the thin whine of machinery started up.

The lift was rising to meet them.

Chapter 7
Cage

Caz held her breath. As the noise grew louder, and nearer, her tension grew.

She had the odd feeling that someone was travelling up towards her. That the someone would be her father. But what if it was something else? Some creature, some monster, from the depths of the earth?

She stepped back from the lift.

The whine grew louder until she could feel it in her teeth and nerves.

Will raised the gun.

Then, suddenly, the cage rose out of the dark in front of them and stopped with a clatter.

It was empty.

Caz breathed out in relief. She felt stupid for being so afraid. She glanced at Will, who lowered the gun with a shrug. Without a word, she stepped inside the cage and he followed, tugging the wire-mesh door shut.

Caz pressed a button on the wall. The cage shuddered and started down.

The light faded until they were standing in a cube of darkness dropping deep into the earth. Caz travelled with her feet planted wide, trying to keep her balance. Will hung onto the metal mesh.

The descent was steady, and fast. Glistening walls shot up past them, gleaming with old seams of coal and ore.

The air grew warm and muggy.

By now Caz couldn't even see her own hand.

And still the cage fell.

"How deep are we?" Will whispered at last.

Caz's voice was quiet over the lift's whine. "Very deep, I think. Five hundred metres, maybe. I –"

The whine snapped off and the cage thudded to a stop. They were at the bottom of the shaft.

They stood in silence and then Will said, "Caz, listen to me. We don't take any risks. We stay together, all the time. OK?"

She nodded, a bit annoyed. Then she pulled the cage door open and they stepped out.

She had expected a low tunnel, but this was higher, like a corridor. The walls were dark and rough, and it stretched out in front of them into the distance. It was narrow, only wide enough for one person to walk down. Dim lights hung at intervals along it.

"Lights!" she said. "Still on! How come?"

"Don't know," Will muttered. "I just wish there were more of them."

The bulbs flickered, and many were so faint that they left deep pits of shadow. Will started to walk, and Caz kept just behind.

There was water everywhere, dripping from the roof and running over their feet. In places it made dark pools they had to wade through.

And there was a smell. Sweet. Mouldy. Unpleasant. Caz couldn't place it.

"What *is* that?" she asked.

Will shook his wet hair. "Who knows? I don't like it."

Neither did Caz, but the smell seemed to grow worse with each step they took. Then, without warning, Will stopped and Caz almost bumped into the back of him.

"Junction," he said.

The space they found themselves in had eight sides and in each side there was an identical tunnel that led away into the dark.

In the centre was a circular control desk, with screens hanging above it, but the screens were dark and wires trailed from them.

Will studied the switches and keyboards.

"Look," he said. "It's all stripped out. As if someone took all the components they needed and just left the rest."

"Needed for what?" Caz said. "You think someone's trying to survive down here?"

"Maybe."

She turned. "We need to find them. We should shout …"

She opened her mouth, but Will grabbed her. "*No!*" he hissed.

Caz shook him off. "If my father is alive …"

"Making a noise is a bad idea. Look." His glove was on the control panel. He lifted it up and she gasped in disgust.

Slime stretched from it.

"It's down here too?"

But even as she said it, Caz realised why the walls were glistening. Layers of slime stretched across them. As if enormous snails had crawled over everything.

She backed off. "I really don't like this. I think we should …"

Will held up his hand. "Wait." For a moment he was very still, concentrating. Then he said, "Caz, listen. I think I can hear something."

They both froze. Caz listened. There was nothing but her own heartbeat, loud in the utter silence of the mine.

Until, very softly, right at the edge of her hearing, she heard a faint sound.

Tap. Tap-tap.

Her eyes widened.

Silence. Then the sound again, tiny as a lost echo.

Tap. Tap-tap.

Chapter 8
Crater

Tap. Tap-tap.

"What is it?"

Will didn't answer. He was listening hard.

"Is it a message?" Caz asked. "A signal?"

"Can't tell."

"We need to go and find it." Caz prowled
the entrances to the eight tunnels. From some
came a cool breath of air, but each led to a black
stillness.

What was down those tunnels?

At the fifth one, Caz stopped to listen. Faint
and far away, the whisper of sound came again.

Tap. Tap-tap.

"This one. This is it."

Will came to stand beside her. "I can't hear anything."

"It's stopped now. But I'm sure it's down here."

Caz walked into the tunnel.

The roof was low. She had to bend her head, then crouch. Her hands touched both sides. She licked sweat from her lips.

Soon she had to crawl on hands and knees.

"This can't be right!" Will muttered behind her.

Caz ignored him. But soon she was wriggling on her stomach, terrified of getting stuck. All she wanted to do was get out of here. She hated enclosed spaces, that feeling of being pressed in, forced in a single direction. The rock above was jabbing into her back and she had to breathe in to get under it.

And then, wonderfully, the space grew.

Caz struggled up to her knees, then stood.

"See anything?" Will whispered. The walls took his words and echoed them into a strange, hollow murmur.

"Not yet. Too dark."

But she could walk again now.

The tunnel descended, so steep that it was hard not to slip. Caz thought she could hear the soft *tap, tap-tap* far ahead, but the shuffles and rustles of their progress were so loud that it was hard to be sure.

They passed a few dark openings on each side.

"I'm keeping straight on," Caz said.

"OK." Will sounded worried. "But I don't like these side tunnels. It's pitch black down there."

The tunnel turned a dark corner and Caz realised that the tapping noise was near. She stretched out her hands and touched something. It was hard, and cold. She shone the torch on it and saw a tangle of metal wires poking out of the wall above what looked like a broken fuse-box. One of the wires was being blown by the breeze from the tunnel.

It tapped loudly against the metal of the box.

Tap. Tap-tap.

Caz stood rigid with disappointment.

Behind her Will made a small sound, a stifled cry. There was a shuffle of feet.

"Unbelievable," Caz whispered. She stepped forward and held the wire, gripping it with her gloved fingers. The tapping stopped. "That's all it was!"

She looked up from the wires. "Will, there's a sort of glow up ahead. There might be something down here after all. I'm not squeezing back through those tunnels, so we may as well go on."

No answer.

"Will?" She turned.

Behind her, the dark passage was empty.

"Will?" She flashed the torch up fast. Light glimmered all over the walls. "Will, where are you?"

The silence of the tunnel was absolute, terrifying. Caz made herself take three steps back. She wished she had the gun.

And then she saw it.

Hidden in the shadows of the rock was an entrance to a side tunnel. It was so low that she had to kneel to peer into it. The muddy floor was all churned up. But the tunnel was blocked by a small metal door.

"Will?" Caz breathed. Her gloved hand was on the door. She knew that if she pulled it away it would be thick with slime.

For a moment Caz's mind was as blank and lost as the darkness of the tunnels. Then she banged on the door.

It shook on its hinges, making a clanging sound, horribly loud.

But it didn't move.

"Will!" she yelled.

Only her own voice came back at her.

And then behind, from down the long tunnel from the eight-sided room, she heard a slow, dragging slither.

She whirled round and flashed the light.

Caz had a fragmented view of something impossible. Caught in the light of the torch was a huge body like a snail, boneless, fluidly rippling. Rust-orange marks striped its sides. Its flesh was an almost-transparent brown. Two pinpoint black eyes swivelled on long, slow muscles.

She swallowed a scream.

The huge moving mass streamed towards her, clogging the tunnel.

Caz turned.

And ran.

Her breath came in gasps and pants. She glanced back in panic and the light from the torch raced crazily round the walls and floor.

She ran so fast she banged and bruised herself. She fell and picked herself up, half sobbing.

But there was light ahead.

Desperate, she scrambled and raced towards it. Whatever was behind her slowed.

Caz felt the tunnel widening around her. With a yell of delight, she ran out into brilliance. She crashed into a metal rail and grabbed onto it, clutching it tight, dizzy and bewildered.

She was standing on a narrow ledge, and far below her, vast and burning and dark, a crater yawned, a great hole in the world.

Plumes of smoke rose from it.

Lava bubbled deep in its heart.

As if once a whole star had come smashing down here, and crashed and burned.

Chapter 9
Mist

Caz took a breath. The cold wind whipped her hair out from her hood. The air was full of smoke and smelled of sulphur.

She pulled on her protective face mask and then glanced back at the tunnel.

The thing – that hideous, slug-like mass – had retreated. As if the light had blinded it, as if it didn't like the daylight.

Caz wiped her gloves on the rail with a shudder. Was that one of the monsters that the woman had been so terrified of? Some huge mutated species? She knew, everyone did, that the Blue Star had had strange effects on animal life. Or maybe the slugs had just grown to that size in the heat and steam of the smoking lava down here.

But Will. Where was Will?

She tried to think calmly. Maybe he had gone behind that tiny door to see what was there, and it had shut on him. But why didn't he answer her? Or maybe someone had dragged him in there and was holding him prisoner, a hand clamped over his mouth.

One thing was sure. Slugs, even mutant slugs, didn't lock doors.

Caz shook her head. She couldn't go back through that closed-in tunnel. She had to find another way.

The wind gusted.

Deep in the crater, the earth bubbled and burst with a hissed explosion.

She stared down at it.

Part of the Blue Star must have crash-landed here. She had learned in her months at the Settlement that the Star had been some sort of comet – certainly it had hurtled towards Earth from outside the Solar System.

When the Star had approached the Earth, chunks of it had broken away under the force of gravity. Many had fallen, some had exploded in the atmosphere. The energy released had been enough to radically change the climate, maybe for ever.

One of those chunks must have smashed out this crater.

The ledge Caz was standing on curved down to become a spiral ramp. She walked along it, her glove rasping rust from the rail. Snow settled in the creases of her coat.

She had to find a way back in! She had to find Will.

But the ramp had no openings, and led only around the edge of the enormous crater. Caz guessed that the miners must have built it in their search for rare metals deep in the smoking, bubbling pit.

She stopped.

What was that she'd heard? She whirled round. High on the opposite side of the crater, mist and steam shimmered in the wind.

Then, snapping out of the grey fog, a bolt of laser-fire drilled into the rock next to her.

Caz yelled and flung herself down.

Another shot of fire melted the metal bar by her face.

"What are you doing!" she screamed. "I'm unarmed!" She wriggled flat, praying the steam would keep her invisible, then gasped as a whole cloud of fluttering black bats rose from the crater, panicked by the noise.

The bats funnelled upwards, round and round. Hundreds, then thousands, of them burst out, a fluttering darkness, swift and silent. They filled the air and blocked Caz from her attacker.

Caz picked herself up and ran as fast as she could back along the ramp. As soon as she moved, another shot drilled at her, but it was way too high, and she knew her attacker was guessing now. But she was running so fast she couldn't stop, and she went crashing hard against the metal rail. To her horror it gave way.

Caz screamed, grabbing at the rail. Her hand slid, then she had hold and was swinging in mid-air, her feet kicking wildly for support, her arms jerking with the effort of holding on.

The black cloud of bats gusted round her, a hissing flutter of darkness.

She couldn't see what was below, but she knew that if she let go she might fall for miles. Her arms were burning as if the muscles would tear apart, and her gloves were slipping off the rail.

She made one last wild swing – and jumped.

She landed with a thud on a pile of snow, all the breath knocked out of her. For a second she lay there, sure she had broken all her bones. Then a shot drilled a perfect circle into the Ice over her head. She swore, wriggled round, and slid.

Caz skidded down the steep slope of snow, but saw that if she kept on she would go right over the edge, into the crater. With a yell of terror she reached out, grabbed a metal bar that was jutting from the Ice, and swung against a metal gate in the wall of the crater.

There was enough force in her swing that the gate gave way and she crashed through.

She slid to a halt, breathless and battered. Then she dragged her knees up under her and stared around in amazement.

Caz was in an ordinary room.

A lamp was burning on a desk. The walls were covered with dark hangings, and there was a bed, a table and a chair, pushed back as if in a hurry.

Caz stood up, turned and closed the door.

Her breath made a soft cloud of astonishment in the air.

There was food on a plate on the table, a half-eaten meal of tofu and rice. Next to the sink a kettle stood. She put her hand on it and drew it back – the plastic was hot.

Someone was living here.

And they had been here only minutes ago!

She bit her lip. Then, on the desk at one side, something gave a warning bleep.

Caz crossed to the desk. She saw a screen showing a hazy image of the crater. The camera must be hanging high above it – steam from the bubbling lava fogged the image.

But she saw someone. A man in a dark overall. With a swift movement she found the zoom and focused in on his face.

It was the same man.

The white-haired guard who had stolen the file from her room. He had a gun in his hand.

So he had followed them here! She frowned, hot with sudden anger, and stepped closer to the screen. The man's uniform was black, and there was an insignia on it she didn't recognise, though she thought she knew all the uniforms of the Settlement.

Fascinated, she looked closer. The insignia showed the Blue Star, exploding in a black sky.

Now at least she knew who her enemy was. And he was far more frightening than the huge, swollen slugs.

Then, on the other side of the door – *Voices!*

Caz shrank back against the wall.

Something slammed and rattled. The door was shaken and thrown open, and before she could move, Will ran in.

Behind him was a man. A tall, very thin man with greying dark hair, who stopped dead and stared at her, wide-eyed.

For a moment Caz couldn't even breathe.

Then she whispered, "*Dad?*"

Chapter 10
Richard

Caz couldn't move. But Richard Lewis could.

He came straight over and wrapped his arms round her so tight the breath was crushed right out of her.

"My God, Caz. I thought you were dead!"

Caz swallowed. Her throat was choked, her eyes blind with tears. "Me too ... I mean I thought you ..."

"You're so grown-up! Will's told me about the years you spent in the City. In that terrible Store. If I'd had any idea ..."

"You didn't. How could you?"

He pushed back from her and she saw that his own eyes were full of tears. "I should have tried! Searched and searched!" he said. "But I never dreamed … All reports said the City was frozen solid, that only wild dogs roamed there." He pushed the hair back gently from her eyes. "Oh, Caz. You look so much like your mother. Like Jenny. I don't suppose …?"

"No," Caz said. "She didn't make it. Only me."

She couldn't stop staring at him. She'd never had any photos, only memories from more than nine years ago, a child's memories, of his big hands, the smell of his woollen jumpers, a tall man kicking a football with her in the park.

He was a stranger and yet she knew him. She could see the guilt and the joy in him. She could see herself in him, for all he said she looked like her mum.

"There's stuff you need to know, Caz," Will said.

Caz nodded. She sat down on the chair and tried to pull herself together, but it was as if a great storm had crashed through her. She couldn't seem to get her breath.

"First check the screen," she said, remembering.

Will looked at it. "It's blank – there's nothing on it."

"There was," Caz told him. "That man with the white hair. He's here! He fired at me!"

"*What!*" Will and Richard said it together. Her father hurried to the screen.

"Are you sure?" Will said. "You saw him?"

"Yes. Look, who is he? What's going on here? What happened on that rescue mission?"

Richard looked worried. "All right. I'll tell you. But we need to hurry. When we got here – the search and rescue team, I mean – the place was deserted. All we knew was that this was a top secret site, not just an ordinary mine. Fran and I suited up and came into the mine. All the power was down. We found the bodies of the miners lying in the tunnels. It looked like some horrible massacre."

"Did those slug things kill them?" Will muttered. "Were they the monsters?"

Richard shrugged. "We thought so, at first," he said. "We'd checked the place out – all the instruments said the air was clear. So Fran took her visor off. I was more cautious. I left mine on."

He shook his head, as if he was trying to shake the horror of his memories away.

"The miners must have hit a pocket of some sort of gas. It was invisible, and toxic, and it didn't show up on any scanner. It worked on the nervous system, on the brain. It gave them hallucinations. Made them imagine things. Drove them mad. Some of them even shot each other, thinking their own comrades were alien creatures."

"How do you know?" Caz whispered.

"Because I saw how it got Fran," Richard said.

"She died?"

He nodded, stricken. "She fell down a crevasse. Running from monsters that weren't there. Screaming, running away from me."

Caz was silent, imagining it.

"What about the others?" Will said. "They were frozen ..."

"I don't know any details. I got trapped down here. Lost in the tunnels. I called and called, but no one ever answered and when I finally got back there I found the plane frozen. All I can think of is total system failure. Or sabotage. As if someone didn't want us to succeed."

"But you must have called for help, right?" Will said.

Richard laughed, bitter. "Of course. For hours. Days. Until I realised no one was listening. No one wanted to hear me. Still, I waited for the rescue party. I've been waiting for over a year. And then I find that the rescue party is you! How …"

"They said you were dead," Caz said. "The file was marked *No further action*."

Her father stared at her in disbelief.

Will was puzzled too. He looked round the dim room. "And you've been surviving here? What about the gas? The slugs?"

"The gas has gone. As for the slugs," Richard said with a shrug, "they're ugly but harmless. There are lots of strange mutations here. Whatever the Star was, it created a lot of new stuff, new elements – including the Eternum. I think that's what this white-haired man is after. We need to get up there before he finds it."

Caz stared. "*Eternum?* That's the word the woman used, on the recording …"

"Right. And it took me a long time to work out what it meant." He grabbed a torch and her hand. "Come on, Caz. You want to know what the Eternum is? I'll show you."

He pulled her with him, and Will followed close behind. They came out into the mists and smoke of the crater.

"This way," Richard said. "Hurry!"

Caz was bewildered by the desolation. The ground was smashed and broken by huge cracks and ravines it would be easy to fall into. Smoke hissed out of them, and the rocks were coated with strange colours, mustard yellow and scarlet and a soft sticky green.

"What is all this?" Will gasped.

"Metals, salts, all sorts of stuff … When the Star fragment hit, they were all thrown up from deep underground, from the very core of the Earth. They reacted with the Star to produce new, unknown elements."

"That's what they were mining?" Will said.

Richard nodded. A spume of gas exploded, shooting into the dark sky. Caz jumped back, against a rock that crumbled and fell at her touch.

"Over here," her father said. "But watch your step. This place is always moving. Nothing is stable."

Caz could see that. She felt she was stumbling across the bottom of a basin that was transforming under her. Steaming cracks opened, and small geysers of hot bubbling mud erupted.

They came to a place where a thin bridge of stone sprang from an outcrop. It led over a deep ravine to the other side.

Richard stopped. "Wait. We need a plan." He turned to Will. "Can you get to your plane from here?"

"I suppose so. But –"

"Get there," Richard cut in. "Radio back to the Settlement. Tell them where you are, that you're bringing back the Eternum. Tell them I'm alive."

Will looked at Caz. "OK," he said. "Then what?"

"Come and get us," Richard said. "We'll be in the chamber."

"Where's that?"

"Up there."

Richard turned and pointed, and they followed his gaze.

High above, almost invisible in the mists of the crater, a spindly spiral structure turned and twisted into the sky.

Caz gazed up at it, with a shiver of awe.

"*The crystal stair*," she whispered.

Chapter 11
Stair

Richard pushed Will. "Go on! We're depending on you."

Will hesitated. He flashed the swiftest look at Caz.

"Be careful," she said, touching his arm with her gloved hand.

He smiled. "Aren't I always?" Then he disappeared into the mists.

"Will he be all right?" Richard asked.

"He's as clever as they come," she said, watching him go.

"Right." Her father turned back to the bridge of rock. "Now. We have to cross this first. Will you be OK?"

Caz thought of the wild dogs back in the City and said, "I've done worse."

But she hadn't.

They walked one behind each other. There was nothing to hold onto. The path narrowed as they went on, and soon Caz could see down past her feet into the depths of the crater. Huge swollen bubbles burst down there. Something soft as lava and red as blood heaved and convulsed. The air was difficult to breathe – it stank of sulphur and a mix of choking acrid smells she could not name.

She pulled her visor back on and Richard did the same.

"Gets tricky now," he muttered.

That was an understatement. The path was so narrow there was nothing of it on either side of her. She walked in air. A fierce jet of steam shot up to her left. When it hit the cold air of the sky it became instant snow, swirling back on her face.

It was an impossible place!

Something bright slashed past her. For a moment Caz had no idea what it was. Then, as her father yelled and staggered and fell, she knew it was gunfire.

"Dad!" she screamed. "He's seen us!"

Richard was sprawled on the narrow bridge, one arm over the side. For a moment, as she flung herself down, grabbed him and turned him over, she was sure that he was dead. Then he opened his eyes and hissed with pain. "I'm OK. I'm OK! It's just my arm."

She helped him up. He hissed again. "*Run!*"

Caz fled across the bridge. Laser-fire slashed her feet. She leaped and landed and ran again. The air sizzled. She ducked, terrified a bolt of flame would drill into her back.

Then the mist came down, surrounding them in a white swirl and she knew they were hidden.

Her father grabbed her, and they stood utterly still.

All around, the crater churned and bubbled. They were right in its heart, on a patch of what seemed like solid ground.

"What now?" she murmured.

"Up," he said.

The mist drifted apart. The crystal stair rose before her.

It was so frail it seemed impossible that it could stand their weight. It was made of something almost as clear as glass, and it glinted like white fire into the sky, as twisted and magical as the beanstalk in the old fairy story her mother had once read her.

"What *is* it?"

Richard was holding his arm tight. "Lava hurled upwards by the explosion, that froze in the air," he said. "It has the perfect temperature and pressure conditions to store the Eternum."

"But what is ...?"

He shook his head. "We have to get up there, Caz. Then you'll understand everything."

He began to climb and she climbed after him. The first steps were wide and pale, hard to see and very slippery. The heat made soft puddles of slush to splash through. The higher they climbed the narrower the steps became until soon they twisted round in such a tight spiral that Caz was dizzy and breathless, her side aching.

Ahead, Richard panted. She glanced down, wondering where the assassin was, but mist had re-covered the crater.

Caz knew that he'd be close behind them.

She forced herself on. Up and up, into the sky. The air grew even colder. The mist above cleared and she could see sudden stars. As she scrambled on hands and feet round the crystal pinnacle she felt as if she was climbing a needle into space, that it was quivering and would snap, and she would plummet down to her death.

Ahead, her father was a dark shadow against the stars.

She stopped and listened.

Somewhere below a soft pattering of steps stopped too.

Was it an echo?

She waited until her father whispered, "Caz!" from above.

Caz ran on.

When the pain in her side was almost too much to bear, she stumbled and put her hands down. She realised she had come to the top.

An archway was cut in the crystal. Caz ducked through it and emerged into a chamber. It was all made of glass and its roof was jagged with hundreds of hanging crystal lanterns that caught the starlight and reflected it. Opposite was another arch, leading out to a tiny balcony, its spindles thin as cord.

Caz gasped in a frosty breath.

In the centre of the chamber, her father stood. He moved aside. "Look, Caz. This is what it's all about."

She came closer.

There was a solid column in the middle of the floor, rising to a flat top. On the very centre of it was a purple glass flask with an ornate silver stopper.

She stared at it. "What *is* that?"

Richard circled the column. "You remember I told you the Star fragment smashed into this place? It created a completely new element. The miners dug it out in secret, and refined it down to this, a few precious drops of liquid. It was so fantastic, so amazing, that they kept it secret from everyone back in the Settlement. Except one man found out ..."

Caz said, "So this is –"

"The Eternum. I found it and brought it here. I finished their work." Richard shook his head. "Though it may have cost us all our lives."

"But what is it?" She came closer, fascinated. She reached out and touched the cool surface of the flask. "What does it do?"

The answer came from behind her, and it wasn't her father's voice.

"*It makes you live for ever.*"

She turned, into the steady muzzle of the gun.

"And I'm here to take it," the white-haired man said.

Chapter 12
Flask

He looked younger, close-up. His face was completely calm. He held the weapon without a tremor.

"Who are you?" Caz whispered.

"You'll never know," he said. "But I'm sorry you got mixed up in this."

Richard took a step forward and the gun swivelled straight at him.

"What are you going to do?" he demanded. "Kill us both?"

The man didn't answer, but Caz knew he would do it. There was a cold calmness about him that terrified her. As if he had no feelings at all. As if killing meant nothing to him.

She moved. Her hand shot out and she grabbed the purple flask and held it tight in her fingers.

"What are you doing?"

"This." She held the flask high. "Shoot me and I drop it. Shoot him and I drop it. Either way, it's gone, smashed to pieces."

The gunman stared at her. "You'll die."

"I don't think we will. I don't think you'll take that risk."

It was a huge bluff. She was fighting to keep her hand from trembling, to keep her voice steady.

For a long moment they faced each other, her eyes fierce on his.

Then, by the tiniest of fractions, he lowered the gun.

Caz flicked a glance at her father. "Is this all there is?"

"It's all I could make."

"And does it really make you live for ever?"

"I don't know what it can do," Richard said quietly. "But I've seen the medical records. None of the miners aged by as much as a day after they came here. They just stopped getting older."

"Enough," the man said. "Put the flask down on the floor."

Caz shook her head.

"Do you think you can get away?" His eyes were hard as flint. "Did you think I wouldn't put your plane out of action?"

She hadn't thought of that. And where was Will?

"Step aside," she snapped. "Or I drop it."

"I don't think so."

"You stole the file," she whispered. "You were in the Pyramid."

"Clever girl."

"You want the Eternum for yourself. You knew it was being mined here, and when the distress message came in you saw a chance to get it."

He didn't flicker.

But a wave of understanding made Caz gasp. "And you closed the file! It was you who wrote – *No further action!* You didn't want anyone else coming out here. You left them to die."

"How …" Richard said.

"He knew you were a chemist," Caz said. "He killed the others and left you here. He knew you'd finish the miners' work. He's been waiting – he knew you'd complete the Eternum. Then he'd come in and get it. Only we got here first."

"Shut up!" The man turned the weapon on Richard. "Give me the flask now. Or your father dies."

"No, Caz! Don't."

She was shaking with tension.

"Give me the flask. Now!" The man's finger moved on the trigger.

In pure fear, Caz yelled, "Take it, it's yours!"

She threw the flask high into the air.

A flash of purple soared under the hanging lanterns of ice. The gunman dropped the gun and grabbed at it, but in the same moment

Richard was onto him, and they were grappling together on the floor for the weapon.

A shadow darkened the starlight.

"Caz!"

She turned and saw the shape of the *Ladybird* hovering outside the balcony. Will brought it in close, the cockpit door open wide. "Jump!" he yelled. "Now!"

She turned back. "Wait!"

"CAZ!"

Richard grabbed the gun and flung it out into the night. "Go, Caz! *Go!*"

She leaped up on the thin railing and dived headfirst into the plane, blanking out the immense drop below.

Her father flung himself in after her, his body smashing into hers.

The gunman scrambled up and hung over the balcony's spindly rails. "I'll find you," he yelled in fury. "The Settlement is a small world. Earth is a small world! *This is not over!*"

But already Will had forced the plane up. It shuddered and shot skywards, the engine screaming in protest. They soared high into the night, a breathless frost blanking the windscreen.

Will said, "Close!", and the cockpit came down on them, shutting out the cold and dark.

Lights flickered in the little red plane.

They were high above the Shadow Valley.

They were safe.

They sat in silence for a while. Then Caz unlatched her visor and took it off, blowing the hair from her eyes. She wiped sweat from her face.

Will watched her for a moment. "You were great," he said.

"I was petrified."

She looked at her father, then he put his unhurt arm round her and she managed a faint smile.

"I thought we were all going to die," she whispered.

He smiled. "So did I, but here I am, rescued by my daughter. I never thought that would happen."

As the *Ladybird* rose high over the world, they saw the Ice rise beneath them, miles of frozen world.

Caz snuggled against her father. She felt utter relief, and yet a strange, heavy sadness.

"Such a shame," she said. "All your work. If that stuff, that liquid – the Eternum – could really encourage growth, prolong life ... think what we could have done with it. We might even have saved the world ..."

Richard nodded. "We might." He lifted his hand. "So I suppose it's lucky I was the one who caught it."

Caz gasped.

Will looked over and laughed in astonishment.

In the warmth of the plane, the purple flask glittered. As the *Ladybird* flew on, it made a bright spark of colour in the darkness.

Far below, for mile on mile, stretched the dim desolation of the Ice.

Our books are tested
for children and young people by
children and young people.

Thanks to everyone who consulted on
a manuscript for their time and effort in
helping us to make our books better
for our readers.

CATHERINE FISHER tells the chilling story of how Caz and Will come to the Settlement in …

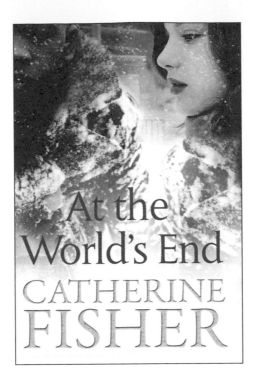

At the World's End
CATHERINE FISHER

The Store is home to a small band of survivors,
who have not set foot outside in the nine years since
the coming of the Star.

Now tensions have reached boiling point, and Caz and Will
are cast out onto the silent, ice-locked streets of the ruined
city. They must make their way to a place of safety, but
have no idea where such a place might be ...

*'Catherine Fisher is one of today's best
fantasy writers'* THE INDEPENDENT

www.barringtonstoke.co.uk